Welcome to ALADDIN

If you are looking for fast, fun-to-read stories with colorful characters, lots of kid-friendly humor, easy-to-follow action, entertaining story lines, and lively illustrations, then **ALADDIN QUIX** is for you!

But wait, there's more!

If you're also looking for stories with tables of contents; word lists; about-the-book questions; 64, 80, or 96 pages; short chapters; short paragraphs; and large fonts, then **ALADDIN QUIX** is *definitely* for you!

ALADDIN QUIX: The next step between ready to reads and longer, more challenging chapter books, for readers five to eight years old.

Read the other books in the Fort Builders Inc. series!

TREE HOUSE STATION

by Dee Romito

illustrated by Marta Kissi

ALADDIN QUIX

New York London Toronto Sydney New Delhi

For our sweet Sienna and Smoky, aka Kitti and Mo ♡

ALADDIN QUIX
Simon & Schuster Children's Publishing Division
1230 Avenue of the Americas, New York, New York 10020
First Aladdin QUIX paperback edition February 2022
Text copyright © 2022 by Deanna Romito
Illustrations copyright © 2022 by Marta Kissi
Also available in an Aladdin QUIX hardcover edition.
All rights reserved, including the right of reproduction in whole or in part in any form.
ALADDIN and the related marks and colophon are
trademarks of Simon & Schuster, Inc.
For information about special discounts for bulk purchases, please contact
Simon & Schuster Special Sales at 1-866-506-1949 or business@simonandschuster.com.
The Simon & Schuster Speakers Bureau can bring authors to your live event. For
more information or to book an event contact the Simon & Schuster Speakers Bureau
at 1-866-248-3049 or visit our website at www.simonspeakers.com.
Cover designed by Karin Paprocki
Interior designed by Mike Rosamilia
The illustrations for this book were rendered digitally.
The text of this book was set in Archer Medium.
Manufactured in the United States of America 1221 OFF
2 4 6 8 10 9 7 5 3 1
Library of Congress Control Number 2021934985
ISBN 9781534452480 (hc)
ISBN 9781534452473 (pbk)
ISBN 9781534452497 (ebook)

Cast of Characters

Eddie Bell: The artist on the Fort Builders Inc. team

Uncle Carter: Eddie's uncle

Noah: Eddie's cousin

Kiara Pal: The designer on the Fort Builders Inc. team

Caleb Rivers: The organizer on the Fort Builders Inc. team

Jax Crawford: The builder on the Fort Builders Inc. team

Naiya: Eddie's sister

Mara: Eddie's cousin

Mr. Greaves: Caleb's neighbor

Contents

1

The Idea

Eddie Bell had been looking forward to five o'clock.

At five o'clock, the workers across the street stopped hammering, hammering, hammering. He could finally do his artwork in peace.

But it also meant his uncle **Carter** and his cousin **Noah** would come over for dinner. They were the ones hammering across the street to fix the Stuarts' roof.

Eddie couldn't wait for family dinner. His dad was making a side of homemade mac and cheese, and Eddie had made banana pudding for dessert.

He was so busy thinking about dinner, he didn't even notice his friend **Kiara**.

"Hi, Eddie," she said.

"Oh, hi," said Eddie.

Kiara was one of his partners in Fort Builders Inc. He and his friends had a business building forts. But Kiara was only in the neighborhood when she visited her grandmother down the street. That's when they had their meetings.

"What are you working on?" asked Kiara.

Clipped to his easel was a photo of a painting. Eddie's canvas had the same bold colors and lots of shapes.

"Jacob Lawrence is one of my favorite artists. I'm trying to paint in his style," said Eddie. "What do you think?"

Kiara took a good look at it. "I

think your paintings will be in a gallery someday," said Kiara. "It's amazing."

"Thanks. What's going on with you?" asked Eddie.

"Well, guess what? I'm staying with Nani all week!" said Kiara. "My parents are going out of town with my brother and sister, but I asked to stay here."

"That's great!" said Eddie. "I didn't even know you had a brother and sister."

Kiara laughed. "They're in high

school, so they mostly hang out in their rooms or with their friends."

Eddie knew all about having a teenage sibling.

"And since it's summer," said Kiara, "we can hang out every day."

Eddie was happy that Kiara would be around more. And he was sure their friends and fellow Fort Builders Inc. partners **Caleb** and **Jax** would be happy about it too.

"And I have an idea," said Kiara. Before she could tell him about it, Caleb and Jax rode up the driveway on their bikes.

"Kiara's staying all week," said Eddie, to update them.

"That's great!" said Caleb.

"More fort building!" said Jax.

"And she has an idea," said Eddie.

They all turned to Kiara.

"I was going to ask Eddie if he could help me design a business card for us," she said, "but I don't know what address to put on there."

Caleb and Jax got off their bikes and kicked down the kickstands.

"So I was thinking, we really should have some kind of office," said Kiara. "Somewhere to keep our supplies so they're not all at different houses."

Kiara was right. They could really use their own space for the business. So far, they'd worked in either Jax's or Caleb's garage.

"My garage is definitely out," said Eddie. "My dad is always working on his own projects." He pointed behind him to a bicycle that had been taken apart.

"My dad is organizing ours," said Caleb. "But right now it's a mess. It'll be a while before we can use it."

"My mom parks her new car in ours now," said Jax, "which doesn't leave much room for us or our supplies."

The kids had helped Kiara's grandmother clean out her garage earlier in the summer. Maybe that was an option.

"I already asked Nani," said Kiara. "But my uncle is moving, so he's storing a bunch of his stuff in there for a while."

They needed to find a place they could keep their supplies. A place their customers could find them.

But where?

2

The Plan

As the team brainstormed plans for an office, Eddie's sister **Naiya** came outside with their little cousin **Mara**.

"I know you're having a meeting, but Mom wants you inside for dinner," said Naiya.

"We're trying to solve a business problem," said Eddie.

"What's the problem?" asked Mara.

"We need an office for our business," Eddie answered. "And we can't use any of our garages."

Mara hopped down the steps. "That's easy," she said. "You need a tree house office!"

"I wish," said Jax.

"But that kind of fort building is a lot more **complicated**."

"Yeah, we'd need adults for a project that big," said Caleb.

Just then, Eddie's cousin Noah walked up the driveway and loaded his tool belt into his truck.

"You mean adults who know how to build things?" asked Naiya. She nodded toward Noah.

Eddie smiled. "Naiya,

you're a genius! And thanks for the idea, Mara! I have the perfect plan."

"Yeah, yeah," said Naiya. "I'll tell Mom you need five minutes."

The team worked quickly on their game plan.

Five minutes later, Naiya came out with another reminder. "Mom says time's up. She wants you to set the table."

"I think we're ready," said Eddie to his team. "We'll put our plan into action tomorrow."

On Tuesday, Eddie spent most of the morning in his kitchen. Kiara, Caleb, and Jax all helped.

He made his famous brownies, of course. He also made the best oatmeal chocolate chip cookies *ever*.

Kiara carefully placed the brownies and cookies into a basket. She folded the flowered napkins just right and added a little note that said ENJOY!

Eddie turned to Jax and Kiara. "You two stay here and watch the last batch of cookies. Caleb and I will go complete our mission."

"Sure thing," said Jax. "As long as we get to taste test them!"

Eddie laughed. "One cookie," he said. "Just let my mom know

when you're ready to take them out of the oven."

Caleb picked up the basket and headed across the street with Eddie to the Stuarts' house.

They had timed it so the workers would be on a break when they arrived.

"Hi, boys. What do you have there?" asked Uncle Carter as he eyed the basket. "It smells fantastic!"

Their plan was already working!

"I brought some of my famous brownies," said Eddie. "And your favorite cookies."

Uncle Carter reached into the basket and took a big bite of one of the cookies. Then he turned around to his crew. "You guys aren't going to believe how good these are!"

Eddie and Caleb waited as the crew munched on the treats.

"You ready for the next step of our plan?" Caleb whispered to Eddie.

Eddie nodded and walked up to the workers. "So we were wonder-ing if you guys could help us with a little project."

"Sure. What do you need?" asked Noah.

"We run a fort-building business, and we could really use an office to work out of," said Eddie.

"A tree house office," added Caleb.

"But we'd need some adults to make it happen," said Eddie.

His uncle reached for a brownie. "We'd love to help, but building a tree house isn't a *little* project."

The boys had planned for that **response**.

"We know," answered Eddie. "But we have a plan. And we're prepared to do a lot of the work."

"We just need you to do the adult jobs," added Caleb.

Eddie handed his uncle the design.

"Kiara is our **architect**. She designs all our forts," said Caleb. "She did a bunch of research and made this in her design app."

Uncle Carter nodded. "I'm impressed," he said. "This is good."

"We'll gather all the materials," added Caleb. "Jax's dad has a ton of extra wood and nails from when their deck was built."

The cookies were almost gone. Noah held up one of the last brownies.

"Will you make us more of these if we help?" he asked.

Eddie smiled at Caleb. That was the final part of their plan.

"Not only will I make you more desserts," said Eddie. "I'll also make homemade pizza for everyone when it's finished."

He hoped that trade would seal the deal.

"You kids understand you'll have to work first before you can play in it?" asked his uncle.

"We do," said Eddie. "We're hard workers."

His uncle smiled and turned to his crew. "What do you think? Are you guys up for a job that pays in brownies?"

"And pizza," Eddie reminded them.

"Count me in," said Noah.

The three other workers agreed to the deal.

"We're almost finished with this job, so we have some time the next couple days," said Uncle Carter. "Can you get all the supplies there by morning?"

"We sure can," said Eddie.

It was time to build a tree fort!

3

Rock, Paper, Scissors

After a short break, the team met at Eddie's porch, ready to build.

Kiara was holding a tin container. "Nani sent these for you." She lifted the lid.

"Ooh, laddoos!" shouted Caleb.

They'd had the treat before, and they were delicious!

"Okay, let's get to work," said Kiara.

There was just one problem.

"We never decided where we'd build the fort," said Jax. "Where should it go?"

"It could go in any of your yards. We

just need a big tree," said Kiara. "Nani's garden takes up most of her backyard."

All the boys had big climbing trees.

"Whoever gets the fort has to get permission from their parents, too," said Caleb.

They'd been so excited about building it, they hadn't thought about the details.

What was the fairest way to decide who got it?

"We have three choices," said Caleb. "What should we do?"

"We can't flip a coin," said Jax. "Rock, paper, scissors?"

"Okay," said Eddie.

Each of the boys made one flat hand and one fist.

As they said the words, they each hit their palm with their fist. "Rock, paper, scissors, shoot!"

Eddie did rock.

Jax did scissors.

Caleb did paper.

Which meant no one won.

"Well, that didn't work," said Kiara. "Try again."

"Rock, paper, scissors, shoot!"

Eddie did rock.

Jax did rock.

Caleb did rock.

"Maybe we need to try something else," said Kiara.

"We should go check out the trees," said Eddie. "Whoever has the tree that fits Kiara's design the best gets it."

They all agreed on the plan.

They walked into Eddie's back-yard. He had a beautiful tree. It was big and tall and full of climb-ing branches.

"That's a good tree," said Jax.

Kiara checked her design. "It would be perfect."

Jax climbed up onto one of the branches. "Yeah, I agree. This is a good—"

But before he could finish his sentence, something buzzed around his head.

"Go away, bee!" shouted Jax,

ducking to get away from it.

But there was another bee.

And another one.

"Get out of the tree!" shouted Caleb. "I think there's a beehive up there!"

Jax twisted and turned and then shimmied his way down the trunk of the tree.

He ran around in circles until he was sure the bees hadn't followed him.

"Well, I guess my yard is out," said Eddie. "Who's next?"

They walked to Caleb's back-yard.

He had a beautiful tree too. It was also big and tall and full of climbing branches.

"Another good tree," said Eddie.

"That would work," said Kiara.

"Check for bees," said Jax.

There didn't seem to be any hives in Caleb's tree.

"I think it's bee-free," said Caleb. "We could build the tree fort here."

A voice came from over Caleb's

fence. "You kids better not be building anything over there," said his neighbor **Mr. Greaves**.

Caleb went closer to the wooden fence. "Why not?" he asked.

Mr. Greaves pointed to a spot in the corner underneath his shed. "There's a litter of kittens under there. They're already scared from all that hammering down the street."

All they could see were five tiny heads—two gray, two orange, and one white.

Mr. Greaves had thirteen indoor cats. And he always made sure any **stray** kittens went to good homes.

"How long will they be under there?" asked Jax.

"They're still very young," said Mr. Greaves. "They'll need to be with the mama cat for at least a few more weeks." He walked back into his house without another word.

"So my yard is out," said Caleb. "Fingers crossed that Jax's tree will work."

"Yeah," said Eddie, "because we're running out of options."

4

An Easier Way

They walked silently to Jax's backyard. It was their last hope.

He had a beautiful tree too. It was also big and tall and full of climbing branches.

Each of them walked around

it and inspected the yard.

"No bees," said Jax.

They walked around again.

"No kittens," said Caleb.

"Jax, where is the extra wood from the deck?" asked Kiara.

"By the shed," he answered.

"So we'll even save ourselves time building it here," said Kiara. "That's definitely a plus."

She was right. It made total sense.

"Is that okay with everyone?" asked Jax. "Caleb, you're only two houses away, and Eddie, you're down the street. We could all use it."

"Sounds perfect," said Eddie.

"Works for me," said Caleb.

It didn't take long for Jax to get his parents to agree to the plan.

It was time to get to work on their tree fort!

They didn't have to move the wood very far, but there was a lot of it to move.

Jax got everyone a pair of

gloves so they wouldn't get slivers. The crew carried the pieces of wood.

"There has to be a better way to do this," said Caleb.

"Yeah, I've never sweat so much in my life," added Eddie.

They all looked to Jax, their master builder. If he didn't have a solution, they'd have to adjust their plan.

"We need to think like **engineers**," he said. "They're professional problem-solvers."

It was quiet for a minute. Kiara
paced back and forth.

"What would make it easier to
move a heavy object?" asked Kiara.

"Something with wheels," said
Caleb.

"Of course! I think I have an

idea," said Jax. "Follow me!"

Jax took off toward the garage, and his friends ran behind him.

Jax's twin sisters, Amber and Dove, were playing with their new kittens in the front window of Jax's house.

"Hi, Kitti and Mo," said Kiara as the kittens climbed all over their pet fort.

The team stood back and admired their latest project, the Happy Tails Lodge. The kittens clearly loved it.

"I'll be right back," said Jax.

A minute later he was inside talking to his sisters.

The team couldn't tell what they were saying, but they seemed to agree on something.

The garage door rose with a loud noise.

Jax came out, rolling a red plastic wagon behind him.

"The girls said we could use this," Jax told the team. "We can put the wood on top and pull it over to the building site."

The crew rolled the wagon to Jax's backyard and loaded up the wood.

"Wow, this is a lot easier," said Eddie.

It still took several loads, but they got it done much faster.

Once the wood was where they needed it, they went back to work getting everything else.

Their neighbors had heard what they were doing and chipped in to help. The team rolled the twins' wagon down the street

for the rest of their supplies.

Miss Nancy gave them leftover cans of paint.

They picked up old shutters from Miss Claudine.

The Fiore family donated a rope ladder from an old play set.

And Mrs. Bott insisted they take some plants to make it green.

Lots of kids were outside playing, but the team had work to do.

Jax had to say no

to a neighborhood game of soccer.

"Maybe this weekend," he said to his friend Greyson.

Eddie couldn't help with a chalk painting kids were doing on the sidewalk.

"Maybe next time," he said to his friend Sage.

And Caleb and Kiara had to pass on a book club their friend Landon was starting.

"We're in for the next one," said Caleb.

After what felt like a gazillion

hours of work, Jax's backyard was full of supplies for the fort.

The team sat back and took a well-earned break.

"I'm exhausted," said Jax, "but I'll be ready for building day tomorrow!"

5

Building Day!

When Eddie's uncle and his crew got there Wednesday morning, the team was ready to build.

There was a lot of "Can you bring me this?" and "Hold that" and even some "Watch out below!"

The kids did whatever was asked of them.

His uncle's crew built a base that **extended** out from the tree. It had support beams underneath to hold up the **platform**.

The frame went up next.

It took all day to get that far, and they still had more to do.

On Thursday, they put up the walls one piece of wood at a time.

Jax helped as much as he could.

Caleb had his notebook the whole time, making sure everything ran smoothly.

Kiara double-checked her design as the fort went up piece by piece.

And Eddie, as promised, brought

the crew trays of delicious snacks. He even made his own strawberry lemonade.

It was a team effort for sure.

There was hammering, hammering, hammering. They hoped it wasn't too loud for the kittens down the street.

Next was the roof. Jax handed supplies to the workers and paid close attention. Someday he'd build a tree fort on his own!

Finally, they secured the railing to the platform.

Safety was important, so Eddie's uncle made sure everything was sturdy and secure.

After what seemed like forever, but also no time at all, the fort was up.

Noah had even built them a small storage shed behind the tree.

"So what do you think?" asked Noah.

"It's all so great!" said Caleb.

"You kids are good helpers," said Uncle Carter.

"I wish we were old enough to build the whole thing," said Jax.

Uncle Carter sat down on his toolbox and wiped his forehead. "Sometimes trading what *you're* good at for what someone *else* is good at is the smartest thing to do," said Uncle Carter. "More gets done that way."

He was right. They had all **contributed** by using their skills, and they had an amazing fort to show for it.

"I can help paint after we eat,"

said Uncle Carter. "And I'll come back tomorrow to get the furniture up there."

But all they could focus on was "eat." They were so hungry.

"Where'd Eddie go?" asked Kiara.

They were about to look for him when he came out the back door of Jax's house in an apron and chef hat. He was holding two pizza trays.

Jax's mom carried a pile of plates and napkins.

"I promised home-made pizza," said Eddie. "Dinner is served!"

Everyone sat down to eat the best slices of pizza in the neighborhood.

"What's your secret ingredient?" asked Kiara. "You always have a secret ingredient."

"True," said Eddie. "But if I keep telling everyone, they won't be so secret anymore."

There was a muffled laugh around the table because everyone's mouths were full.

"Thank you so much," Eddie said to his uncle's crew. "You can come to our office anytime you want."

Uncle Carter laughed. "I'm not sure I'll make it up that rope ladder."

The pizza was delicious, but dinner was interrupted when Uncle Carter got up to take a phone call.

After he hung up, he walked back to the table. "I'm really sorry, but we have to go," he said. "One of our customers has a roof emergency."

Eddie wasn't sure exactly what that meant, but he did know they wouldn't have help painting.

"It could be a couple weeks before I can finish the tree house," said Uncle Carter.

But they only had a couple days before Kiara had to go home.

. . .

After they cleaned up dinner, the Fort Builders team climbed up the rope ladder into their new fort.

"We could leave it like this," said Jax. "It's still a cool fort."

It was. And they could. But they didn't want to.

"It'll look so much nicer painted," said Eddie. "It should be colorful."

Kiara agreed. "And we want to show our customers that we're serious business owners."

Caleb stood up. "So let's paint

it," he said. "If we can build castles and pet forts, we can figure out how to paint a tree house."

"You're right!" said Jax. He climbed down the ladder and went into the shed. He came out a minute later with a bunch of painting supplies.

"Everything's here?" asked Kiara. "I thought it was all in Noah's truck."

"He put the supplies in the shed earlier," answered Jax.

"Okay, team," said Kiara. "Let's get this finished before my parents come home on Saturday. I want to be able to play in it!"

"That's plenty of time," said Caleb. "We have two days."

The group sorted through the supplies.

"How do we get these heavy paint cans up there?" asked Jax.

It was hard enough to climb a rope ladder when you *weren't* carrying paint!

"We could use a pulley!" said

Eddie. "We can pull our supplies up to the fort. I'm sure my dad has one we can use."

Eddie ran home. Sure enough, his dad had just what they needed.

They set up the pulley, attached one paint can at a time, and pulled them up with the rope. Then they attached a basket for the rest of the supplies.

Jax poured the blue paint into the trays. They each grabbed a brush or a roller and started painting.

It was hard work, and after a while they took a short water break inside the tree house.

But they would run out of time if they didn't get back to work soon.

Out on the balcony, something was different, though.

"Uh, I think we have a little problem," said Kiara. She pointed down.

All along the platform were two sets of little blue paw prints.

6

Paw Prints

They followed the paw prints across the balcony, down the tree, and through the grass.

Caleb pointed to the open sliding glass door.

"Kitti and Mo must have gotten

out!" said Jax. "My dad will not be happy if they get paint all over the new deck."

"Or in the house," added Kiara.

The team peeked under the deck where the prints had stopped.

Staring back at them were two pairs of big, round eyes.

"Come here, kitties," said Jax, trying to get them to come out.

He reached underneath, but they backed up farther.

"Where'd Caleb go?" asked Eddie.

Caleb came down the steps with a bag of cat treats and two old towels.

"This is how you get a cat to come out," he said. He handed Jax and Eddie the towels. "Get ready." He shook the bag. "Who wants treats?"

In no time at all, Kitti and

Mo ran out to get the treats. Blue paws and all.

Jax and Eddie wrapped them up in the towels.

"We have to clean that paint off their paws before they lick it and get sick," said Caleb. "Looks like painting the tree house will have to wait."

On Friday, after making sure Jax's kittens were inside the house, they finished painting the tree fort. They decided to leave the little blue paw prints. Eddie thought they made it extra special.

Eddie also painted some colorful designs on the inside walls.

On Saturday, once the paint was dry, the team met up to add the finishing touches to their fort.

Caleb wanted to put books on the shelves, and Eddie wanted to keep some of his art supplies in the tree house.

"I'd love to store my sketches and clipboards here," said Kiara.

"We can use a basket for that," said Jax. "But what about the big stuff?"

Kiara grabbed her clipboard. "What if we use more **simple machines**?" she asked the group. "Like the pulley and the wagon. They're **devices** that make work easier."

"Great idea!" said Caleb.

Eddie grabbed a sheet of paper and drew the six simple machines they'd learned about in school—wheel and axle, lever, inclined plane, pulley, screw, and wedge.

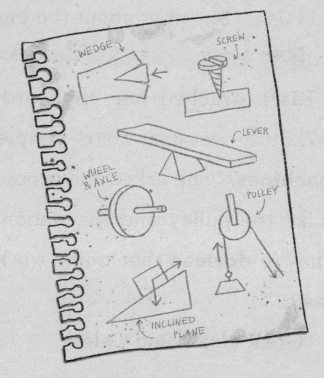

Jax pointed to Eddie's drawing. "We could use a ramp to push the heavy stuff up there."

"Let's do it!" said Kiara.

Jax and Caleb ran off to get a flat piece of wood to make a ramp.

They set the bottom of the piece of wood on the ground and lowered the top onto the platform at an angle.

"Perfect!" said Caleb.

"Now we just have to get everything up there," said Eddie.

Kiara and Caleb went up on

the fort balcony. Eddie and Jax pushed up a box of Caleb's books, a rug, two chairs, and a small table.

The next step was to get the plants, Eddie's art supplies, and Kiara's clipboards into the fort. They added them one at a time to the basket, and Kiara and Caleb pulled the rope to bring it to the balcony.

"Grab it, Caleb," said Kiara.

He reached for the basket, but it tilted too far away from him.

One of the plants landed on the ground with a splat! "Try it again," said Caleb. "I'll balance it better this time."

Between the ramp and the basket, they managed to get everything into the fort.

They placed the chairs and table in the perfect spots, lined the books on the shelves, and neatly organized the supplies.

Once everything was in place, they climbed down, removed the ramp, and stood in front of their creation.

"It's amazing!" said Eddie.

"It's so beautiful!" said Kiara.

"I can't believe we did it," said Caleb.

"That's a beauty of a fort," said Jax.

After nearly a week of hard work, the friends' new Fort

Builders Inc. office was ready.

Almost.

"I'll be right back," said Jax.

Within minutes, Jax was running back into the yard.

He hung a wood sign on a nail.

"It's great, Jax!" said Kiara.

"Thanks," said Jax.

"One more thing," said Caleb. "I have a secret project I've been working on. Come on, I'll show you!"

They walked to Caleb's house, and he told them all about it.

Very quietly, they walked up to Mr. Greaves's front porch. Caleb set a gift bag in front of the door.

"Do you have the note?" asked Jax.

Kiara put the note card on top of the bag. Although they'd secretly named the backyard kittens Mocha, Buddy, Sweetie, Pumpkin, and Marshmallow, the note simply said FOR THE KITTENS with a big heart on the side.

Eddie had also slipped their new business card in the bag with a little message on the back.

PET BED IN OFFICE. KITTENS ALWAYS WELCOME.

They rang the doorbell and ran behind a bush. Their parents had taught them not to do that kind of thing as a trick, but they wanted this to be a surprise.

Mr. Greaves stepped
outside and looked
around. He noticed
the bag, read the
note, and pulled
out one of the cans
of kitten food.

Then he smiled.

"Do you think
he knows it's from us?" asked
Eddie.

"Maybe," said Caleb. "But at
least he knows someone cares."

As soon as the coast was clear,

they bolted down the street to Jax's backyard.

"This fort was really fun to build," said Jax. "But I'm so glad we're done."

They all laughed and then climbed up into the fort.

"Time to celebrate our hard work, crew," said Caleb.

The Fort Builders Inc. team sat back and relaxed . . . in their brand-new office tree house.

Word List

architect (AR•kih•tekt):
Someone who designs buildings

complicated (KOMP•lih•kay•tid):
Complex or advanced

contributed (kuhn•TRIB•yoo•ted):
Provided help

devices (dih•VYE•sez): Objects
or machines made for a specific
purpose

engineers (en•juh•NEERS):
People who design things and
solve problems

extended (ik•STEN•did): Stuck out from a main point

platform (PLAT•form): A raised, flat surface

response (rih•SPONS): A reaction or reply

simple machines (SIM•puhl muh•SHEENS): Devices with no or few moving parts that make work easier

stray (STRAY): Having no home

Questions

1. The Fort Builders Inc. team decided not to build their fort in three of their yards. How did this show respect for others?

2. Building the fort was hard work. What did the team do to make some of the work easier?

3. Many characters in the story were generous with their time and their things. Who showed generosity and how?

4. If you built a tree house fort, what would it look like?

STEM Activity

How to make an inclined plane racetrack:

Step 1: Use a piece of sturdy cardboard or a piece of wood, or cut a pool noodle or wrapping paper roll in half. Have an adult help you with cutting the items!

Step 2: Attach one end to a table or bookshelf and the other end to a box on the floor.

Step 3: Roll a toy car, marble, or bouncy ball down the inclined plane and time it from start to finish.

Step 4: Move the track higher and time it again.

Step 5: What do you notice about the time it takes for the car or ball to reach the end each time the track is raised?